The books in this series introduce young children to the four rules of number.

This book gives over one hundred basic facts of division. The lively, colourful cartoon pictures illustrate the number bonds and mathematical symbols are used under each picture. There are hours of fun and learning for all young children who love counting and simple arithmetic.

Published by Ladybird Books Ltd Loughborough Leicestershire UK
Ladybird Books Inc Auburn Maine 04210 USA

Printed in England

PRACTISE AT HOME

Fun with DIVISION

written by ROGER and MARY HURT
illustrated by LYNN N GRUNDY

6 ÷ 2

Ladybird Books

We share four shoes between two boys.

Each boy has two shoes.

$$4 \div 2 = 2$$

We share two hats between two girls.

Each girl has one hat.

$$2 \div 2 = 1$$

We share six apples between two boys.

Each boy has three apples.

$$6 \div 2 = 3$$

We have no apples to share between the two girls.

They each have no apples.

$$0 \div 2 = 0$$

We share eight bananas between two monkeys.

Each monkey has four bananas.

$$8 \div 2 = 4$$

We share ten nuts between two squirrels.

Each squirrel has five nuts.

$$10 \div 2 = 5$$

Count down in twos.   Can you do these sums?

10
8
6
4
2
0

$10 \div 2 =$ $10 \div 5 =$

$8 \div 2 =$ $8 \div 4 =$

$6 \div 2 =$ $6 \div 3 =$

$4 \div 2 =$

$2 \div 2 =$ $2 \div 1 =$

$0 \div 2 =$

Try to learn these facts.

| 10 | 8 | 6 | 4 | 2 | 0 |

We share six shoes between three boys.

Each boy has two shoes.

$$6 \div 3 = 2$$

We share three hats between three girls.

Each girl has one hat.

$$3 \div 3 = 1$$

We divide nine bottles between three houses.

Each house has three bottles.

$$9 \div 3 = 3$$

If we have no bottles to share,

each house will have no bottles.

$$0 \div 3 = 0$$

If we share eight wheels between
four cycles,

each bicycle has two wheels.

$$8 \div 4 = 2$$

If we share four wheels between
four cycles,

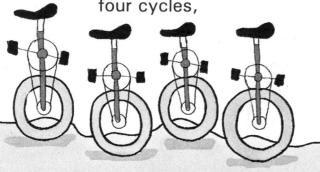

each cycle has one wheel.

$$4 \div 4 = 1$$

If we divide twelve wheels between four cycles,

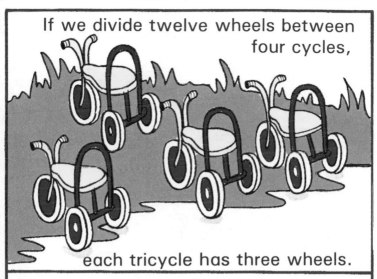

each tricycle has three wheels.

$$12 \div 4 = 3$$

If we divide no wheels between four cycles,

each cycle has no wheels.

$$0 \div 4 = 0$$

Which fish are caught in the nets?

If we share sixteen pencils between four boys,

each boy will have four pencils.

$$16 \div 4 = 4$$

If we divide twelve pencils between four boys,

each boy will have three pencils.

$$12 \div 4 = 3$$

What are the missing numbers?

$4 \div \bigcirc = 2$

$12 \div \bigcirc = 6$

$\bigcirc \div 4 = 3$

$\bigcirc \div 4 = 0$

$9 \div \bigcirc = 3$

$10 \div \bigcirc = 2$

$\bigcirc \div 4 = 1$

$12 \div \bigcirc = 4$

$\bigcirc \div 3 = 0$

$16 \div \bigcirc = 4$

Try to learn these facts.

If we share fifteen flags between
five sandcastles,

each castle will have three flags.

$$15 \div 5 = 3$$

If we divide fifteen flags between
three sandcastles,

each castle will have five flags.

$$15 \div 3 = 5$$

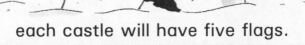

If we share twenty stamps between four envelopes,

each envelope will have five stamps.

$$20 \div 4 = 5$$

If we divide twenty stamps between five envelopes,

each envelope will have four stamps.

$$20 \div 5 = 4$$

Here are twelve buttons.
If we place them in four rows,

there are three buttons in each row.
We can say 12 ÷ 4 = 3

If we place the buttons in three rows,

there are four buttons in each row.
We can say 12 ÷ 3 = 4

Here are twenty apples.
If we place them in four rows,

there are five apples in each row.
We can say 20 ÷ 4 = 5

If we place the apples in five rows,

there are four apples in each row.
We can say 20 ÷ 5 = 4

Count down in threes.

Can you do these sums?

Count down
15
12
9
6
3
0

$15 \div 3 =$ $15 \div 5 =$

$12 \div 3 =$ $12 \div 4 =$

$9 \div 3 =$

$6 \div 3 =$ $6 \div 2 =$

$3 \div 3 =$ $3 \div 1 =$

$0 \div 3 =$

Try to learn these facts.

15	12	9	6	3	0

If we share twenty-five sausages between five children,

each child will have five sausages.

$$25 \div 5 = 5$$

If we share five sausages between five children,

each child will have one sausage.

$$5 \div 5 = 1$$

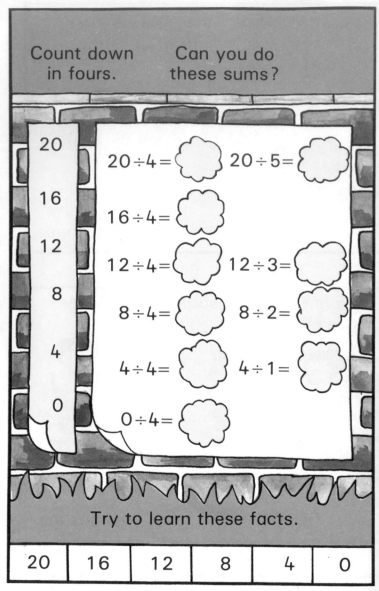

Count down in fours.

Can you do these sums?

20
16
12
8
4
0

$20 \div 4 =$
$20 \div 5 =$

$16 \div 4 =$

$12 \div 4 =$
$12 \div 3 =$

$8 \div 4 =$
$8 \div 2 =$

$4 \div 4 =$
$4 \div 1 =$

$0 \div 4 =$

Try to learn these facts.

| 20 | 16 | 12 | 8 | 4 | 0 |

If we share eighteen flowers between six vases,

each vase will have three flowers.

$$18 \div 6 = 3$$

If we divide twelve flowers between six vases,

each vase will have two flowers.

$$12 \div 6 = 2$$

Which clowns are holding the balloons?

10 ÷ 5

6 ÷ 6

8 ÷ 8

15 ÷ 5

18 ÷ 6

12 ÷ 6

1   2   3

Count down in fives

Can you do these sums?

| 25 |
| 20 |
| 15 |
| 10 |
| 5 |
| 0 |

25 ÷ 5 =

20 ÷ 5 =   20 ÷ 4 =

15 ÷ 5 =   15 ÷ 3 =

10 ÷ 5 =   10 ÷ 2 =

5 ÷ 5 =   5 ÷ 1 =

0 ÷ 5 =

| 25 | 20 | 15 | 10 | 5 | 0 |

26

If we share twenty-four cakes
between six children,

each child has four cakes.

$$24 \div 6 = 4$$

If we divide six cakes between
six children,

each child has one cake.

$$6 \div 6 = 1$$

If we have thirty eggs
to put into six boxes,

each box will have five eggs.

$$30 \div 6 = 5$$

If we have thirty-six eggs
to put into six boxes

each box will have six eggs.

$$36 \div 6 = 6$$

What are the missing numbers?

15 ÷  = 3

24 ÷  = 6

 ÷ 6 = 5

10 ÷  = 2

 ÷ 6 = 0

18 ÷  = 3

20 ÷  = 4

 ÷ 6 = 4

6 ÷  = 6

25 ÷  = 5

Try to learn these facts.

Count down in sixes.

Can you do these sums?

36	$36 \div 6 =$
30	$30 \div 6 =$ $30 \div 5 =$
24	$24 \div 6 =$ $24 \div 4 =$
18	$18 \div 6 =$ $18 \div 3 =$
12	$12 \div 6 =$ $12 \div 2 =$
6	$6 \div 6 =$ $6 \div 1 =$
0	$0 \div 6 =$

36	30	24	18	12	6	0

If we divide twenty-one fish between seven bowls,

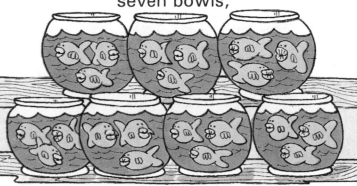

each bowl has three fish.

$$21 \div 7 = 3$$

If we divide fourteen fish between seven bowls,

each bowl has two fish.

$$14 \div 7 = 2$$

If we divide twenty-eight buttons
between seven coats,

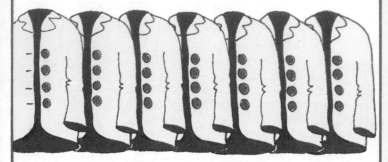

each coat has four buttons.

$$28 \div 7 = 4$$

If we divide forty-nine buttons
between seven coats,

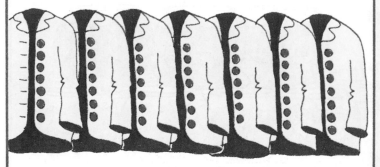

each coat has seven buttons.

$$49 \div 7 = 7$$

If we divide thirty-five pencils
between seven pots,

each pot will have five pencils.

$$35 \div 7 = 5$$

If we have no pencils to divide
between seven pots,

each pot will have no pencils.

$$0 \div 7 = 0$$

If we share forty-two medals
between seven soldiers,

each soldier will have six medals.

$$42 \div 7 = 6$$

If we share seven medals
between seven soldiers,

each soldier will have one medal.

$$7 \div 7 = 1$$

Count down in sevens.

Can you do these sums?

49	$49 \div 7 =$	
42	$42 \div 7 =$	$42 \div 6 =$
35	$35 \div 7 =$	$35 \div 5 =$
28	$28 \div 7 =$	$28 \div 4 =$
21	$21 \div 7 =$	$21 \div 3 =$
14	$14 \div 7 =$	$14 \div 2 =$
7	$7 \div 7 =$	$7 \div 1 =$
0	$0 \div 7 =$	

Try to learn these facts.

| 49 | 42 | 35 | 28 | 21 | 14 | 7 | 0 |

If we divide thirty-two candles
between eight cakes,

each cake has four candles.

$$32 \div 8 = 4$$

If we divide eight candles
between eight cakes,

each cake has one candle.

$$8 \div 8 = 1$$

If we divide sixteen books
between eight shelves,

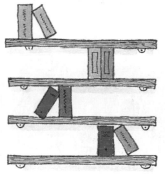

each shelf has two books.

$$16 \div 8 = 2$$

If we share fifty-six books
between eight shelves,

each shelf has seven books.

$$56 \div 8 = 7$$

If we divide forty-eight strings between eight guitars,

each guitar has six strings.

$$48 \div 8 = 6$$

If we divide twenty-four strings between eight guitars,

each guitar has only three strings.

$$24 \div 8 = 3$$

Can you do
these sums?

64	$64 \div 8 =$
56	$56 \div 8 =$ $56 \div 7 =$
48	$48 \div 8 =$ $48 \div 6 =$
40	$40 \div 8 =$ $40 \div 5 =$
32	$32 \div 8 =$ $32 \div 4 =$
24	$24 \div 8 =$ $24 \div 3 =$
16	$16 \div 8 =$ $16 \div 2 =$
8	$8 \div 8 =$ $8 \div 1 =$
0	$0 \div 8 =$

64	56	48	40	32	24	16	8	0

If we divide forty rings
between eight pegs,

each peg has five rings.

$$40 \div 8 = 5$$

If we divide sixty-four rings
between eight pegs,

each peg has eight rings.

$$64 \div 8 = 8$$

What are the missing numbers?

$14 \div$ $= 2$

$24 \div$ $= 3$

$\div 7 = 6$

$8 \div$ $= 1$

$21 \div$ $= 3$

$\div 8 = 0$

$35 :$ $= 7$

$40 \div$ $= 8$

$49 \div$ $= 7$

$\div 8 = 8$

Try to learn these facts.

If we divide sixty-three eggs
between nine nests,

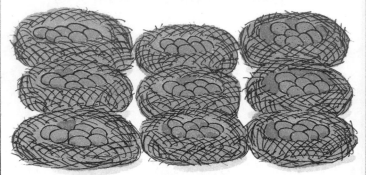

each nest will have seven eggs.

$$63 \div 9 = 7$$

If we divide nine eggs
between nine nests,

each nest will have one egg.

$$9 \div 9 = 1$$

If we divide eighteen arrows between
nine quivers,

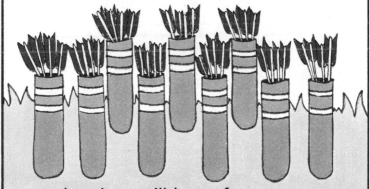

each quiver will have two arrows.

$$18 \div 9 = 2$$

If we divide thirty-six arrows
between nine quivers,

each quiver will have four arrows.

$$36 \div 9 = 4$$

Which apples fall into which baskets?

If we divide twenty-seven sandwiches
between nine plates,

each plate will have three sandwiches.

$$27 \div 9 = 3$$

If we divide fifty-four sandwiches
between nine plates,

each plate will have six sandwiches.

$$54 \div 9 = 6$$

If we divide forty-five cherries between nine cakes,

each cake has five cherries.

$$45 \div 9 = 5$$

If we divide eighty one cherries between nine cakes,

each cake will have nine cherries.

$$81 \div 9 = 9$$

Count down in nines.

Can you do these sums?

81
72
63
54
45
36
27
18
9
0

$81 \div 9 =$

$72 \div 9 =$ $72 \div 8 =$

$63 \div 9 =$ $63 \div 7 =$

$54 \div 9 =$ $54 \div 6 =$

$45 \div 9 =$ $45 \div 5 =$

$36 \div 9 =$ $36 \div 4 =$

$27 \div 9 =$ $27 \div 3 =$

$18 \div 9 =$ $18 \div 2 =$

$9 \div 9 =$ $9 \div 1 =$

$0 \div 9 =$

81	72	63	54	45	36	27	18	9	0

What are the missing numbers?

$72 \div$  $= 8$

$32 \div$  $= 4$

 $\div 6 = 9$

 $\div 9 = 0$

$56 \div$  $= 8$

$36 \div$  $= 4$

 $\div 4 = 8$

$24 \div$  $= 3$

$8 \div$  $= 1$

$18 \div$  $= 9$

Try to learn these facts.